UPDOG

DANGEROUS JOBS

ICE ROAD TRUCKERS

CLARA CELLA

Lerner Publications ◆ Minneapolis

Lerner Publications Company
An imprint of Lerner Publishing Group, Inc.
241 First Avenue North
Minneapolis, MN 55401 USA

For reading levels and more information, look up this title at www.lernerbooks.com.

Main body text set in ITC Franklin Gothic Std.
Typeface provided by Adobe Systems.

Library of Congress Cataloging-in-Publication Data

Names: Cella, Clara, author.
Title: Ice road truckers / by Clara Cella.
Description: Minneapolis : Lerner Publications, [2023] | Series: Dangerous jobs (updog books) | Includes bibliographical references and index. | Audience: Ages 8–11 | Audience: Grades 4–6 | Summary: "Without ice road truckers, people in the coldest regions of the world wouldn't be able to survive. Learn about brave journeys across frozen roads, and see how truckers stay safe to deliver the goods"— Provided by publisher.
Identifiers: LCCN 2022014745 (print) | LCCN 2022014746 (ebook) | ISBN 9781728475547 (library binding) | ISBN 9781728486215 (paperback) | ISBN 9781728481869 (ebook)
Subjects: LCSH: Truck drivers—Juvenile literature. | Ice crossings—Juvenile literature. | Trucking—Arctic regions—Juvenile literature.
Classification: LCC TL230.3 C424 2023 (print) | LCC TL230.3 (ebook) | DDC 629.28/44—dc23/eng/20220622

LC record available at https://lccn.loc.gov/2022014745
LC ebook record available at https://lccn.loc.gov/2022014746

Manufactured in the United States of America
1 – CG – 12/15/22

Table of Contents

DEEP FREEZE

The ice road trucker drives slowly. He has miles to go. If he drives too fast, the ice beneath him may crack.

Ice road truckers work in cold places. They drive rigs on roads made of ice.

rig: another name for a semitruck

They carry food, fuel, and other goods to people in faraway places.

Ice roads cross frozen bodies of water. Truckers face snowstorms and extreme cold.

extreme: beyond usual

Rigs rarely break through the ice. But they may break down or roll over.

UP NEXT! HOURS ON THE ROAD.

LONGEST ROAD

The world's longest ice road goes through Yellowknife, Northwest Territories, Canada. Truckers first drove it in the mid-1950s. They carried supplies for diamond mines.

mine: a pit from which minerals or other substances are taken

BIG RIG CLOSE-UP

Ice road truckers need big, powerful rigs.

SEMITRUCK

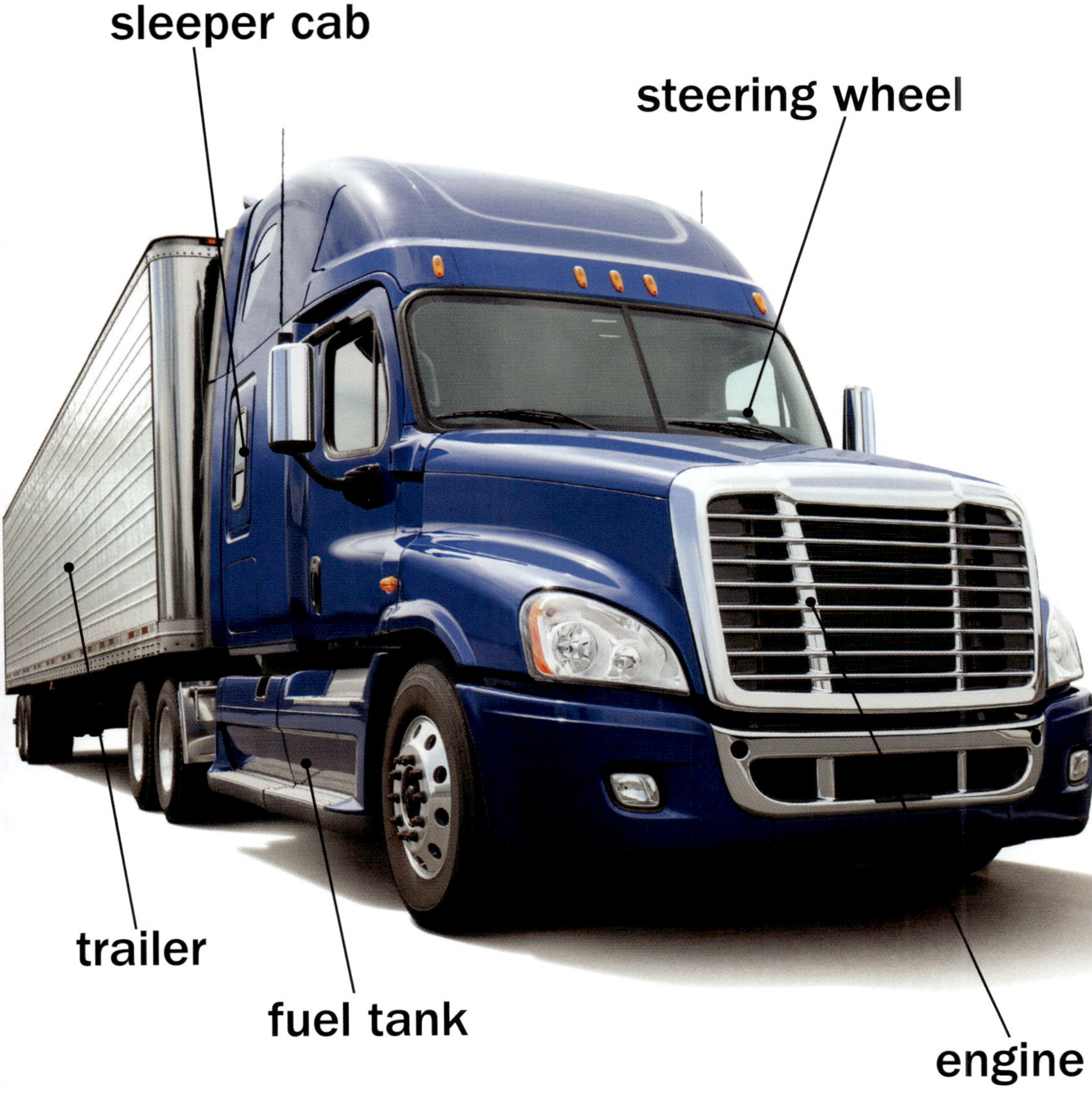

Truckers still use the Yellowknife ice road. But they drive more advanced trucks and carry larger loads.

advanced: better developed

Truckers deliver everything people need for one year in just a few months.

UP NEXT! MELTING ICE.

DRIVE SMART, BE SAFE

Ice road truckers train to drive safely.

They learn to care for their rigs.

Climate change makes ice roads freeze later and melt earlier.

climate change: a long-lasting change to Earth's weather patterns

Truckers have less time to drive each year. They make less money and deliver fewer loads.

Ice road truckers have tough jobs. But they help people get the supplies they need.

MEET AN ICE ROAD TRUCKER

NAME: Alex Debogorski

BACKGROUND: Debogorski grew up on a farm in Alberta, Canada. He became a truck driver at the age of 19.

CLAIM TO FAME: Debogorski starred in the popular reality TV show *Ice Road Truckers* from 2007 to 2017. In 2010, he wrote a book about his life on the ice road.

Glossary

advanced: better developed

climate change: a long-lasting change to Earth's weather patterns

extreme: beyond usual

mine: a pit from which minerals or other substances are taken

rig: another name for a semitruck

Check It Out!

Britannica Kids: Truck and Trucking
https://kids.britannica.com/students/article/truck-and-trucking/277434

Honders, Christine. *Truck Drivers*. New York: PowerKids, 2020.

Kiddle: Semi-Trailer Truck Facts for Kids
https://kids.kiddle.co/Semi-trailer_truck

Kiddle: Truck Facts for Kids
https://kids.kiddle.co/Truck

Manley, Erika S. *Truck Drivers*. Minneapolis: Bullfrog Books/Jump!, 2018.

Rea, Amy C. *Ice Road Truckers in Action*. Mankato, MN: Child's World, 2017.

Index

Photo Acknowledgements

Image credits: Image by Nonac_Digi for the Green Man/ Getty Images, p.4; Splash News/Newscom, p.6; Grundsteins/ Shutterstock, p.7; Lucas Payne/Newscom, p.8; JessicaHarrison/ Getty Images, p.9; kozmoat98/Getty Images, p.10; Bruce Yuanyue Bi/Getty Images, p.11; Image by Nonac_Digi for the Green Man/Getty Images, p.12; stockstudioX/Getty Images, p.13; ryasick/Getty Images, p.14; Geo Swan/Wikimedia, p.15; Alistair Berg/Getty Images, p.16; gk-6mt/Getty Images, p.17; kali9/Getty Images, p.18; Karen Deatherage/Bureau of Land Management Alaska, p.19; Hugh Rose/DanitaDelimont. com/"Danita Delimont Photography"/Newscom, p.20; fullvalue/ Getty Images, p.21; Splash News/Newscom, p.22

Design Element: Mega Pixel/Shutterstock

Cover: Piu_Piu/Shutterstock